BY

MARIAH EMANII

TABLE OF CONTENTS

CHAPTER 1

This bitch was bugging out. She had all of my clothes strewn all over the yard. When I tried to ask her, what was going on all she would do was look at me intensely and wag her finger no.

"Well, can I at least see the children?"

"You can't see a motherfucking thing," she scolded me. Instantly I went into beg mode.

"Cherie why are you acting up. Girl quit playing," I said to her.

"Omar ain't no one playing. Take your shit, get the fuck out of my house and DON'T even think to call me in the morning."

"Seriously baby? Seriously?"

"Yes, seriously and I ain't your baby. Reserve that title for the secret babies you have on the way." "*Aww fuck,*" I thought to myself. She done went and found out about Geneva.

"Baby, I don't have any babies on the way. The only children I have are the ones that you birthed."

"Nigga, do I look like a got-damn fool to you? Matter of fact don't answer that. Just know I've seen the text messages."

"*Got damn, Geneva lied and told me she deleted me out her phone. Now Cherie is telling me this dumb shit,*" I thought to myself again before speaking. "Listen Cherie. Let's just calm down, go in the house and talk things over."

"You are never allowed in my house again. You can see the kids outside, in your car, or at your momma's house, but you will never step foot in my shit once again. And I mean that."

"Baby, please it's not what you think. Yea, I fucked up one time and hit Geneva's ass, but she threw that pussy at me baby. Now that I realize what trash she is she wants to come and tell you these pitiful lies."

"Save it, I saw the doctor's visit that you went with her. I know the sonogram shows you are having twins, a boy and a girl. I know that you said one day you would finally leave me and you and her and your children would live together. I'm tired Omar. So tired. I tried my best to make you love me and only me, yet you don't reciprocate any type of affection or respect towards me. There is but so much a woman can take from a man. A man that she's been with since high school. A man that she has four children from. I've let myself go and not only do you not want me, but no man in their right state of mind will want me either," she said looking defeated. It broke my heart. I know that I love my children's mother. I love the family life she has made for me. She keeps a clean house, cooks and fucks me whenever I need or want to. She may have some love handles but it is nothing to be self-conscious over. When she gets dressed to go out with her sisters I sit at the front room window until I see her car lights pull in the driveway. I'm jealous over my wife and I know that she got those love handles because she birthed children, my children and I love her. I feel so ashamed. She sounds so broken and it's all my fault. My wife is my backbone. Not only that she is the perfect package, but there's this dog in me that won't let me be faithful. Now I know that this might sound like a cop out, but it's true. When it comes to women I'm like a kid in the candy store and have to purchase more than just the chocolate kit-kats, I needed the almond joys, nutter butters, and the milky ways. It may sound fucked up, but I was in love once before her and come to find out the girl that I was loving on fucked my best friend behind my back. Her name is Carmen and she was one of the popular girls. All the boys wanted to date her, and the girls were jealous of her. I wasn't as popular as her, but that didn't stop me from shooting my shot and when she accepted I was elated. I worked an after-school gig and would spend the majority of my check buying her little trinkets and getting her nails and feet done. Then I found out she fucked my best friend, Willie. What a shock. I felt like a knife had been stuck in my chest. I broke it off with her and cut Willie off as well. I haven't spoken to any of them since. Then I met Cherie and she was everything that Carmen was not. She was wholesome, loyal and she submitted to me and doted on me too. I felt good when I was around her, but part of me couldn't get over the hurt that my first true love put me through.

"Hello, Omar, do you hear me?"

"Nah, I'm not hearing you. I'm going to take my clothes and put them back in the house. Don't you ever bring up another woman to me again. I love you, I worship the ground you walk on and I'm not going to lose you because of a quick lay I got from another bitch who couldn't hold a candle to you. Do you understand me?"

"Sounds good, but no, I don't understand you. If you loved me so much, then why hurt me in the first place? Why cheat on me? Why make children outside of our home? I mean you have given me your ass to kiss on so many different occasions but this one takes the cake. Maybe you don't want to hear this, but I'm tired of you and your lies. I deserve better and by goodness I'm going to get better. Now take your shit and we can arrange your visitations with the children at a later date." With that said she turned on her heels and walked back into the house slamming the door behind her. I was left in the yard looking stupid as the neighbors peeked out their blinds.

"What the fuck are you all looking at? Don't act like you don't live in a glass house. I swear people are going to be the death of me," I screamed while picking my shit up from off the lawn. I gathered as much of my stuff I could carry and threw them in the trash bin. I do not want these clothes anymore I simply have to buy a new wardrobe. I walked back over to my car, got in and drove aimlessly around the city. I needed time to cool off before I decided to go back to Geneva's house. She was in for a big surprise when I whoop her ass for getting me in hot trouble with my wife. Now, normally I'd call any man who hit a female a punk, but my adrenaline is pumping. I have come to realize that sometimes women take a man to that boiling point and I was there. I drove back to my home and took one more look at it. I saw Cherie's shadow move and the curtain slip back into its rightful place. My heart dropped with the curtain. I blew the horn a few quick times and I saw her peek again. I saw my baby girl Zera jump in the window and heard her scream, "Daddy's home."

"Get away from the window now Zera. Your daddy ain't walking his narrow ass through my front door," Cherie screamed. I blew on the horn a few more times and Cherie came to the door.

"Get the fuck out of here before I call the police. Now in this day and age I'd hate to call them, but you've gone too damn far," she bellowed.

"I love you," I yelled back.

"Love a dog's dirty dick, you maggot," came flying out her mouth and stabbing me in my heart. I looked at her and told myself, *"Just give her some time."*

I wanted to tell her so many things but instead I opened my mouth and all that came out was, "Have the kids dressed tomorrow in the early afternoon. I'll take them for ice cream or something," and I drove off leaving her there with her hand on her hips staring after me. I know she was hurt and now I was too. It was going to take a while to get over it.

CHAPTER 2

CHERENE 'CHERIE' ROBERSON

My man meant the world to me, but he has a serious problem named dogvitis. Yes, dogvitis is a real thing. For no matter how good a woman treats a man he has to go out in the streets and fuck around with any bitch in heat. Now as for my man, he wasn't like this in the beginning. He was cordial when courting me then after I became pregnant with my first child, he started to fuck any thing moving. I smelled the different perfumes lingering on his clothes and saw the lipstick on his collar. One time he just didn't give a fuck and had lipstick on his draws. Sometimes I would say something and other times I looked the other way. I didn't want to give up on my family and after every time he cheated, and I confronted him he'd treat me like a queen for a little while. But now, he's having children outside of our home with another female. I have nothing against any girls he used to fuck with. I know they don't owe me loyalty; he does. However, that is the one thing he couldn't seem to give to me and I just can't take his shenanigans anymore. He's hurting me too bad and it's all too often. I stay in the relationship with the hope that things will go back to the way things used to be, but it never seem to. Due to this last incident I am padlocking my heart, changing the locks on the door and removing his name off of our joint bank account. I'll be damned if he wine and dines another bitch with money that I contributed to him and his success. That's another straw that's breaking the camel's back. I helped him out with getting his degree in the pharmaceutical field. I worked my ass off learning bookkeeping and also became a pharmacist assistant so that when he opened his pharmacy he wouldn't have to hire anyone outside of our family. Whatever money we made was poured back into the business and he didn't have to pay me a salary because I knew all the profit was coming back to us in our joint account. There wasn't a Simpson left unturned on our part, but with the good came the bad and with the beauty came the beast. He started staying out late nights and that's when my eyes started to open up to all his devilish ways. I chose to put up with it so many times that now I'm serious and he thinks

I'm playing around. I can't, and I won't come in second fiddle to no bitch no matter how young or how old. After Geneva left my house upon telling me she was fucking my husband I politely thanked her for informing me of his infidelities, put her ass out of my house, raced around the house gathering everything that belonged to him from CD's, DVD's, Radio equipment, clothes and sneakers and started to throw them out the front door. I went as far as to douse some items with gasoline, but he pulled up during midstream of my tantrum and tried to sweet talk his way back into my house, but I'm fed up, so he can have his little side bitch become his main bitch, but I know one thing, I will never have any more woman friends in my life. If you didn't catch it, Geneva was a friend of mine. Not my best friend, but we were cool, we kicked it whenever we saw each other, went to get our nails done together and even enjoyed a movie and drink or two with each other. The bitch even met my sisters. Now how I'm gonna look in their eyes. I'm so upset that it took all of this for me to realize she was probably just scheming on my man. Fool me once shame on you but fool me twice then shame on me and I hated to be shamed. So, he has to go, and she doesn't have to worry about me calling or contacting her either. Hell, if I hadn't been pregnant I would have fucked her ass up, but just like her I am pregnant again. I just found out and Omar doesn't even know yet. I'm sure if I told him he'd play on my sympathies again and find a way to stay in our marital home. Speaking of which I am glad I took his name off the deed of our house. When I die there's no need for him to have this place. I didn't want any bitches in my house. Not even his mother, since she raised a sorry excuse for a man. My house goes to our eldest child Januvia and if Januvia isn't of age then it goes to my youngest sister as she is named guardian of the children. It's only right I provide a place for them to reside.

"You're going to regret this," Omar said to me breaking me from my current thoughts.

"Not as much as you probably do right now," I retorted.

"Oh really?" he asked sounding a bit surprised that I was being flip at the mouth which he wasn't used to. He was used to the crying me. The one who begged and pleaded to know what was so wrong with me that he couldn't remain faithful. Not the me that was throwing his clothes and his ass out of my home.

"What you don't understand English now? You fucked up, I'm putting you out and I'm not fucking with you any longer. Simple!"

"Nothing is that simple. This is partly my house too. If you want me to leave you have to formally evict me."

"Speaking of which, this house isn't partially yours anymore," I smirked.

"What? What do you mean?"

"I had your name taken off the deed. There's nothing you can do about it, since you signed the paper a while ago."

"Huh? Cherie, stop playing with me. This IS partially my house and I don't have to leave, but you must formally evict me."

"That's what you think?" I laughed.

"It's not what I think, but more like what I know."

"Well, then you should know that when I had you sign some papers I said were for the mortgage on the house was really a paper signing your part of the home to me therefore taking your name off of the deed. Cherene Roberson is now the full and rightful owner of this house. And it's Cherene Roberson that says you must leave."

"You didn't. I don't believe you."

"Oh yea, yes I did. Would you like to see the new deed?" "Of course," he remarked causing me to dig into my bra and pull out the photocopy of the deed.

"This is a photocopy. Where is the real deed?"

"The real deed is in a safety deposit box at my new bank. And oh yea, I withdrew all the money from our joint account and deposited into my new single account."

"Cherie stop playing. We saved over $300,000 in that account."

"I'm not playing, and you are right, we did save over $300,000 in that account. I'm not completely heartless I did save you SOME of the money."

"Whew, I was about to say how can you leave me destitute like this, but you saved me some money. I hope you saved me half the money."

"Hahaha, Half? That's a joke, right? Did you give those bitches half the dick? Especially Geneva? Did your punk ass give her half?" I asked swinging at him as I spoke. I missed nearly every hit I took but the last one connected surprising us both. After regrouping Omar continued to try to sweet talk me.

"Stop playing baby. This isn't about another bitch but what's rightfully mine."

"Nothing is rightfully yours. I'm the mastermind behind all your endeavors and I was the one that held down the shop while you played out in the streets and in other bitches bed, so because of suffering and pain, I took out around $200,000 and left a one-hundred thousand to help you get back on your feet. Also, the pharmacy has been sold. The selling price was $500,000 and wait there's hope. I did leave you a bit of the profit."

"Which is?"

"I left you another $100,000.00. See baby that's $200,000.00. I'm not completely heartless."

"A hundred-thousand dollars. Man, what am I supposed to do with that? I can fuck up most of that in the mall no problem."

"If you were wise you'd invest in yourself by buying some dope and flipping it."

"Now you are bugging Cherene."

"Oh your using my government name, I must have truly made you upset. Huh Omar? Did I make you upset? You won't have nothing by the time those babies are born, and you and your new baby momma can struggle together like you and I did in the beginning of our relationship. I mean since she wants to be me and all. Have all the things that I have then she can have my former struggle. I'm too good to whoop her ass physically so I'm going to fuck with her mental. You have nothing, you are nothing and you will always be nothing. Do you hear me motherfucker," I now said screaming with spittle flying from my mouth and hitting him all up in his face. I started throwing wild haymakers again. I saw his face and he didn't look hurt enough. I wanted him to hurt the way I was hurting. The way I've been hurting. I wanted him to hurt for eternity like I would be. All he looked was a bit nervous and I gave him my verbal assault even harsher. I talked about his knock-kneeded momma, his junky ass father, his whoring sisters and even talked about his great, great granddaddy. I mean I went full flip mode on his ass with my mouth.

"Let me get my ass out of here," he said defeated.

"Wait, there's more," I screamed at his back causing him to cease walking.

"More?" he asked bewildered.

"Yes, more…5…4….3….2…1…. here comes more," I screamed and giggled like a little kid on Christmas day as the repo truck pulled up and started to hook Omar's brand-new 2018 Mustang to its bed.

"Wait, now you are not playing fair. You know that car means the world to me. I bought it off the showroom floor."

"And I thought I meant the world to you, but see how you did me? So, things that mean the world to you aren't really a thing because the only person or place that you care about is carrying your twins and her name ain't Cherie."

"Here we go with this Geneva shit. I told you she was just a ho that I fucked once or twice, and those babies aren't mine. "

"Yawl had a whole relationship. But if you disrespect the mother of your children I can only imagine how you would disrespect me to others. I mean I know the truth, but anyway. This little conversation is over. You did what you did, and I did what I did. Every action has a reaction and you should know that."

"Baby, please let's just go in the house and talk about this," he begged.

"Naw, but to show you I'm not totally heartless you can call me in about two days. I'll probably be open to have a discussion with you."

"Are you sure honey?"

"Please do not call me honey, boo, bae, baby or sweetheart. Those are all names you called your mistress and I don't need to be reminded of this."

"Sure, anything you ask Cee. I hope in two days you'll be ready to work things out with me. I'm not willing to let you go yet and I hope you feel the same."

He went in for a kiss and I tensed up.

"Damn, you don't love a nigga no more? I mean I can' t even kiss or hug you without you cringing. This shit really hurts."

"Well, it's your own damn fault now isn't it?" I replied.

"I'm going to win you back. I mean that."

"Whatever. Would you like me to call you an Uber? I'm tired of looking at your face."

"Nah, I'm good. I'll just walk to the cab stand around the corner."

"Whatever floats your boat. Peace."

"Peace," he replied then went through the gate and toward the cab stand. As much as I was upset in this moment I felt some sort of relief. Then the tear ducts overflowed, and I was crying freely with tears streaming down my face. Part of me still loved Omar, but part of me loved myself more. I know at the rate he was cheating on me pretty soon we'd contract an incurable STD and my health wasn't something I cared to play with. I wanted to be alive and healthy for my babies. Something Omar knew nothing about.

My phone started ringing and I didn't recognize the number. Instead of sending it to voicemail I answered out of curiosity.

"Your man's here," Geneva taunted me.

"Well if he's with you why bother me? I mean really are you 14 or 35? Which one is it because I can't tell."

"Listen you old hag."

"Hey, where is all this hate coming from? I listened to you and put him out yet you're still bothering me. If you wasn't pregnant I'd dog walk your ass."

"Bitch you couldn't see me on your best day."

"Geneva, we both know you are a punk. I mean Melissa small ass dog walked you all through Patterson park. You didn't even get one hit in. That fight was the funniest and sorriest thing I've seen in a long time. Now you behind a phone trying to act hardbody."

"Bitch, if I wasn't pregnant, I'd…."

"Blah, blah, blah. You are doing way too much talking for my taste. After you drop your load come holler at a player and watch I smack the shit out of you."

"Whatever, MY man is coming in the room now I'll speak to you later after I fuck his ass to sleep."

"Yo, who are you on the phone with," I heard Omar asking. I rolled my eyes and started to chuckle.

"Bitch what the fuck is so funny?"

"You and YOUR man, you can have him. I'm done with him. I mean seriously I am done with him."

"Bitch if you don't want me to call your phone anymore then change your number."

"Why should I? You aren't that important," I said then hung up the phone and surprisingly I didn't feel anger, but peace. A peace which I haven't felt in a while. It was over for Omar and I and I am honestly okay with that. Now if Geneva don't grow the fuck up I'mma hurt her ass. Seriously.

My phone rang again, and it was the same number Geneva just called me from.

"Bitch you won. He's yours. I'm out of the picture. Now that that's established can you stop playing these little girl games on the phone?"

"No, you don't want to play games, but I do, and I am not going to stop calling you. If you want me to stop then change your phone number."

"Who the fuck are you to tell me what I should be doing. If you continue to call here I will have you face harassment charges and I don't care about the outcome. Maybe you'll have the babies while behind bars."

"Your narrow ass would do that wouldn't you?"

"Damn, straight, I don't owe you shit, so yea, I don't have a fuck to give once you are arrested for stalking me."

"Bye snitch."

"Bye miserable bitch and remember, I'll fucking have you arrested and I don't care about you or Omar or your children. Now that niggas broke let's see how much longer you'll love him."

"Huh? He's broke?"

"If you can huh you can hear!!"

"He owns a whole pharmacy and you claiming he's broke?"

"I sold the pharmacy, the house, repoed his car and stripped his bank account naked. There's nothing left from him to profit over and he is probably only staying with you because his funds have run out, but nice try. He's your problem now," I said then hung up in her ear. She called back a few times and I sent her calls straight to voice mail. She left numerous messages threatening me and telling me what a sorry excuse of a wife I was. The next day I politely went to the police precinct to press harassment charges and spoke to a detective about the harassing phone calls and the driving by my home honking the horn. He told me not to worry he will contact her today and tell her to cease all forms of communication with me. I thanked him for his services and left out. My cravings were kicking in, so I made a left turn on to Metropolitan Avenue intending to go to the nearest Baskin Robbins and ordering a shake made of butter almond ice cream when I saw a car nearly clipped my side. I had to do a double take. "Geneva," I whispered and thought to myself, "What the fuck this bitch want she won Omar so why is she still stalking me? Utterly confused I figured I better call my family and let them know what was going on in case this bitch was really unstable and got stupid and really wound up trying to kill me. My sisters were pissed to say the least. They promised a Roberson ass kicking if I just said the word and that's when I had to remind them that the bitch was pregnant.

"Damn, that nigga really got that bird bitch Geneva pregnant, huh?" my sister Charee asked.

"Word, that nigga fucking that bird and without a condom. Sis I hate to tell you this, but you need to go get tested for all types of H.I.V. and even the package. Humph, humph, humph," my sister Cherise said putting in her two cents.

"Alright ladies. I will. I'm tired and just want this shake so that I could go home to my babies and put my feet up and relax.

"You want us to come out there now. You shouldn't be alone seeing as homegirl is tripping like this."

"Nah, I'm good for now," I said but truth was I was doubtful.

CHAPTER 3

GENEVA BLUNT

Wouldn't you know it, I see Cherie as I was going to get my daily dose of chocolate fudge from Baskin Robbins. I was warned to stay the hell away from her by the detective. Yep that dog went and snitched on me to 12 but I wanted the bitch to acknowledge my presence, so I clipped the side of her car and kept it pushing.

When I got home sort of pissed that I couldn't get my chocolate shake with the hot fudge, I replayed Cherie and my last conversation in our mind. This bitch done got rid of Omar and left his ass broke in doing so. Now he's sleeping at my house and not contributing to any bills. This is totally not the man that I wanted. The man I wanted was a young black business man who'd throw the money at me. Now he doesn't have anything to give and I'm here five months pregnant with his twins. I don't want to go back to work, but want the life that Cherie had. She was able to take care of the family businesses and bookkeeping duties. She seemed to run a tight ship but that's what kept him dripping in the finest jewelry and dressed in the latest gear. Now she leaves him and it's just my luck he's destitute. I'm so upset I don't know what to do. I started to wonder if Cherie had any life insurance policies which named him the beneficiary. If she did then I could go ahead and arrange for her murder. He can cash in on the life insurance and we'd be living in the lap of luxury again.

"Hey what are you daydreaming about over there," Omar asked me as he shoveled another large spoonful of Corn Pops cereal in his mouth. The way he ate used to be cute to me, now he disgusts me, and I don't think it's the pregnancy hormones either. This nigga's broke and instead of trying to find a way out of the hole he dug for us he rather sit in the house all day, eat my food and play video games.

"Boy some prize," I slipped and said aloud.

"What was that? I didn't hear you," he said shoveling more cereal in his mouth.

"Nothing honey," I lied, "go ahead and finish up your cereal."

"Is there something wrong. I've been sensing an attitude coming from you?"

"Honestly?"

"Stop playing of course I want honesty."

"You are what's wrong with me. When I took you in it was because not only do you need a place to stay, but I thought you would contribute to some of the bills around here."

"So, all the times that I did contribute to this household means nothing?"

"I didn't say that, but that's the past. I need to know what you are going to be able to do here especially when the twins are born."

"Well bitch, you the one who made this bed now you get to lie in it."

"What? How the fuck you figure that?"

"Were you not the one who went and told my wife everything? Did you think that she was that stupid to let me go with everything she has worked so hard on building? Now I know at one point I was able to contribute to your bills, but you know in all honesty you get what you deserve. Had you just kept your mouth shut we wouldn't be in a financial hell hole. You wanted me all to yourself AND THAT's why you told my wife what you did. You had to know things wouldn't be too easy for us."

"I didn't think that you'd be broke, but here you are. Broke and destitute. Haven't had a hair cut in what seems like weeks. I don't want a man I have to take care of."

"Listen I have a few hundred I could throw your way, but you are going to have to pull most of the weight around here until I figure something else out. Please just bear with me and I promise things will only improve. Things can't get worse than this and if they do then I can always go stay at my mother's house."

"If you say so, but you don't have to go. Just figure something out. Anything has to be better than this," I said hesitantly. Everything in me wanted to believe him wholeheartedly, but my mind knew my heart was wrong. It was like I was the subject of an old R& B song.

"What are you thinking about Pumpkin? Trust me everything will be fine. I can put my degree to use and find another pharmacy to work at until I save up enough money to finance opening my own."

"I mean isn't there something you can do? How can she just sell everything from under you?"

"Well, I signed the papers and I can try and say that it's not my handwriting, but it is, and any plagiarist expert will attest that it is. So, it seems everything on her end is legit. I'm just going to have to go back to working for someone until I can get my own. Things won't be too bad. We can use the new minivan I just bought you to get us around from point A to point B until things turn around in our favor. But don't fret everything should be on the incline in about three months."

"But the babies are due in four months. How's that enough time to save up money? I'm tempted to send your ass back to her just, so you can find a way to steal back what's rightfully yours."

"Sorry, she's still the mother of my four children. I'm not going to just steal from her. That would put my children in a horrible bind and that's something I REFUSE to do. If you can't understand that then like I said earlier I can leave and probably go to my mother's house for a spell."

"You're not going anywhere. I'll struggle it out with you, but you have three months to make something happen. You can start looking for jobs for next week, but right now I want to enjoy you. Got any Xans?"

"Come on, why are you being such a pill head. Do you know the affects that drugs can have on those babies?"

"Just one big daddy, I promise that this will be the last time."

"But you said that the last time. I don't want any fucked-up children addicted to prescription pills because momma didn't know how to sacrifice until they were born."

I looked at Omar like he had one hundred heads. He knows that part of me stayed with him because he had access to the good drugs, but now not only is he broke, he doesn't have the connection to the drugs like he used to. This is going to be rough.

"What are you thinking about?"

"Oh, nothing much."

"Spill it!"

"Well, you know. I just need to pop a pill."

"Not for four months and if I catch you high off of ANYTHING, I'm going to personally kick you in your ass and leave you. Do you understand?"

Rolling my eyes, I said, "Of course I understand. I understand that by telling your wife about us fucked up what we had going on."

"See, I told you to be patient, but no, you couldn't even do that. Now look at the jam we are in."

"Well this jam better hurry up and clear up or I don't know what I'll do."

"That's the withdrawals talking and it's best that you get this part over with, so we can move on and live a sober life until those babies are born.""You're right baby. I just get wound so tight at times without my pills."

"Well you better get used to it because there will be many more nights of not being able to get what you want."

"Well if you give me some money I can go to my old connect and get hooked up."

"Speaking of your old connect, can I do business with him? I have some pills, no not Xans, that I need to get off. If I do everything correctly they should buy us a cool $45,000.00. How's that sound to you?"

"Perfect baby. I knew you'd come through with something tangible, but what pills do you have laying around if they are not Xans? Percocet's?"

"Yes, Percocet's and no you cannot have one."

"Oh, just one won't hurt. I promise I'll never underestimate you again," I said with my fingers crossed under the table. Seems I have been underestimating him all this time. How can he be so stupid to sign papers given to him without reading what they were pertaining to? I mean I know Cherie is his wife and all, but that still shouldn't stop him from reading the papers. Now he learns the hard way what not reading documents before signing them can do. It's just too bad that I have to suffer with him. "Ah well, what's done is done. I just need to know how to get some pills before the nights out or I'm going to be one mean raging bitch," I thought to myself.

"Hey dreamer. There you go zoning out. Is there anything I can get you? Are you and my babies hungry baby? I can chef you up some cheese eggs, grits and turkey sausages."

"Sounds delicious. Can we have some buttermilk biscuits with butter and jam with that?"

"You can have whatever you like."

"Hmm, so besides the food are you on the menu? Because that's what I really want. Some nice hard dick to get me through this rough patch."

"After you eat, I'll give you some back shots. Would you like that baby?"

"Of course, that's my favorite position."

"Good, mine too. I can hold your ass down and keep you from running from the dick," he said causing me to chuckle. His beefcake is juicy and when he hits it from the back I get all types of weird sensations. Most times I try to get out from him pinning me down by my shoulders and all he'd say was, "Take all of daddy's dick." And to tell the truth I loved every minute of it.

"I see that smile starting to show up. That's what I'm talking about. Let me make you happy baby."

"Oh, don't worry. I'm happy," I said as I watched Omar run around the kitchen trying to put breakfast together. "There's also no need for you to rush around baby. It's not like you have to leave and make it home on time so that wifey doesn't become suspicious. You're my husband now and some of the rules have changed. You hear me Omar?""Yes, I hear you loud and clear. It's just going to take a few minutes to become adjusted to living here and not at home with Cherie. I'm sure I will get used to it in time, but for now, the wounds are fresh."

"Damn, she hurt your feelings that bad that you are talking about wounds and shit?" I said giggling. "If I knew this was going to be such a hassle I would have kept my big mouth shut. Now look what I got us into," I said and noticed the dark and gloomy look lingering in Omar's eyes. I swear they pierced right through me and my soul. It's like he hated me or something and unless I was mistaken it looked like death was in his eyes. I made a mental note not to trust him too much and also to refrain from talking about Cherie and his kids. For all I know he could be upset with me and want some revenge no matter how sweet he was acting. Chills coursed through my veins at the mere thought that he hated me.

"You know what? Can you bring the food to me in the bed when it's ready?"

"Why what's wrong?""I suddenly don't feel too good. I think it best if I go lay down."

"Must be morning sickness."

"Must be."

"Sure, go lay down and try to relax baby. I'll be up there in five minutes with your plate give or take a few minutes.

I looked at him deeply. "God, I love this man," was all I could think of. Then the reality that he didn't have a job or anything to contribute to the household's needs and I automatically hated the decision I made to go and tell Cherie about me and Omar, but I wanted him to myself. Yet, I didn't want, nor did I think, I'd get the baggage that came with him. In order to have some sort of income I'll introduce him to my connect and see if he can let off some of those pills and I'll also take a little bit for myself as well. I crossed my fingers behind my back and prayed silently to God to allow Omar's moves to be fruitful; I needed a hit. I was jonesing bad. I was beginning to feel restless and my legs started to shake into overdrive. I noticed Omar staring at me and shaking his head disapprovingly. I felt as if his actions were belittling me, but I didn't want to argue. I made a mental note to search his things when he either took a shower or went to sleep and see if I could find his stash. If I could get one pill to take the edge off then going through the rest of the withdrawal stage should be easy.

CHAPTER 4

I know I'm acting all sweet and shit when it comes to Geneva. Trust me this is just an act. I hate the fact she ran her mouth to my wife and now I have to live here in her studio apartment. For those who don't know what a studio apartment is it is simply an open space equipped with a kitchen and small bathroom. It's like living in a compact living room. I mean she has it decorated nicely in red, gold and with African sculptures, but there's no room for a big man like me with some children. The worse part is it's in the Projects. Now I'll fuck with project people, but I don't want to live in the projects. I did that growing up with my mom who was a single mother. That's why I worked hard and became educated doing something I loved so that my wife, myself, and my children had a roof, other than the projects, over our head. The arrangement Cherie and I had was perfect and I usually don't let my philandering ways affect my home. Now here comes Geneva ruining shit for me. That's why I'm putting all types of different pills crushed into her food. I don't want to kill her because I mean the bitch has some good pussy, but I don't want any children with her and the pills I crushed should help her ass miscarry. Call me what you like, I truly don't give a fuck, but there's only one woman I want to carry my child and that's Cherie. I will not accept outside children in my home. Now this is a big change of heart because the idea of Geneva having my twins was a welcomed addition as long as she knew and didn't pass her place which she did when she told my wife about them. Now I'm damn near destitute and have to perform tasks that I took an oath not to do and that's sell some of the inventory from the pharmacy. Hopefully, we don't get caught making this sort of transaction. I know I'm taking a big chance because the way Geneva like to run her mouth sometimes exacerbates me and have me wanting to stick a knife through her throat.

But that would be too easy and lead back to me. Geneva has a record of being an addict. So I can make the twins death look like it was her fault. I looked over towards where she was lying to see if she were looking at me. When I was confident that I was in the clear, I pulled out the baggie of crushed pills and sprinkled some in the pot with the grits in it. When I was satisfied that I put in a good amount of drugs in the grits I started to make her plate. I heaped the grits on added butter and salt and pepper the way she liked them then added the turkey bacon, turkey sausage, biscuits and eggs to the plate. Instead of jam I gave her sausage gravy which I poured more crushed pills into and let them simmer in the pot. I poured her a cup of freshly squeezed orange juice and brought her plate and cup to her. I pulled up a television tray and took her plate from her and sat it on the tray.

"Sit up and eat all this food. You are eating for three not two, so you better eat all of this," I said sternly.

"Looks and smells delicious baby. You forgot to bring my fork."

"Oh, hold on let me go get that." I rushed to the kitchen area and grabbed eating utensils. I brought them to her and placed them on the tray. She started to eat, and wouldn't you know it she started to eat the grits first.

"Hmm, you did something new to these grits?""Nah baby. Same grits, same recipe and same way I have always been cooking them."

"I can't put my finger on it, but they taste different; good but different."

"Different in a bad way?" I asked becoming a bit annoyed that she just wouldn't shut up and eat.

"No, definitely taste different, but not in a bad way."

"Okay, so eat up. You need your strength."

"Sheesh I don't know if I should eat all this food. I think the itis is setting in already. I feel tired."

"Well eat what you can and I'll either put the rest up for you later or throw it away and make something else for dinner later on."

"Yea, I'll take a new dinner because reheated grits doesn't taste too Kosher."

"No worries. What do you want for dinner so that I can take the meat out of the freezer?"

"I can go for some fried chicken with mashed potatoes and creamed corn."

"Sure thing," I said then got up and went to the kitchen and looked through the freezer. I found a bag of chicken wingettes and took them out, placed them in a bowl and sat the bowl in the sink filled it with water and sprinkled a bit of salt into the water so that the meat could defrost faster. I watched Geneva intently as she laid down and snuggled under the covers. I didn't feel too sorry for her or the babies she was carrying. If only she would have kept her mouth shut. But see that's the problem with these new age side chicks. They want to take the place of the main chick, but don't have sense enough to keep their mouth shut and let the main chick position die out. There were times I was ready to leave Cherie, but I had too much invested in her plus I really love her. However, given a chance and the fact that if Geneva never showed her true colors I might have left Cherie for a spell, but nope, Geneva went and threw a monkey wrench in the game. What she doesn't know though is that I'm not totally broke. I have been stashing money on the side in a safety deposit box. Don't ask me how I got the money past Cherie's nosey ass. Well I might as well let the secret out, I mean what else do I have to lose? In order to get more money, I became a plug to a ring leader of an illicit gang named The Crypt Keepers. They sold pills, heroin and powder cocaine to junkies down by 149th street and Third Avenue in the Bronx. And because of that I'm not totally busted. I have about $400,000.00 stashed away in a bank, but Geneva is greedy. I can see it in her eyes. That's why those babies have to die. I don't want to be tied to Geneva for the next eighteen years of my life. Once I'm satisfied that the babies aren't viable, I'm leaving her ass and going to Philly for a while. I secured a job with a person I went to college with. After I save up $800,000.00 more I will be able to open up my own pharmacy and that's why I need Geneva's connect because my salary at the Philly pharmacy plus with the leader of the gang will take too long to save up for my own inventory. While my life seems to be in shambles I do have some workable options. I just have to remain focused.

"Come here Omar," Geneva screamed making me think something was wrong with her. "What's wrong baby?"

"Nothing's wrong. Feel my stomach; the babies are moving."

"Just great," I thought to myself. I gave her belly a little pat and said, "We have more than enough time for me to feel them move. Let me go finish prepping the food."

"Sure, please do not use too much salt, I don't want my pressure to rise seeing as I just got it under control. The doctor says I'm at risk for preeclampsia."

"No worries," I said grateful that she gave me another option to do what needed to be done. I could mix a lethal dose of salt and these crushed pills. Maybe it will bring on her preeclampsia. My mind started to wander in a million different directions.

"Hey, don't sit here and fall asleep without putting the food on to cook," she said gently.

"Oh shoot. I was so comfortable I almost forgot about cooking," I lied through my teeth. Lying was becoming a habit but who cares as long as it meant I'd get what I wanted in the long run.

I went in the kitchen and started to check her spice cabinet. I saw Lawry's Season Salt, Adobo and Sazon con achiote. I rinsed off the half way defrosted chicken and began to sprinkle all three seasonings on the chicken. Once I was satisfied that I put enough I sprinkled a bit of the crushed pills and began to mix the chicken around to absorb the white powder. I placed the large dutch pot on the stove and added cooking oil to it. I turned the flame on high and waited for the grease to heat up. Once it did I added the chicken after shaking it in some flour and watched my concoction cook. I made the mashed potatoes from real potatoes and then realized we didn't have creamed corn so corn on the cob would have to do.

Once the food was cooked I made Geneva's plate and sat it on the kitchen table. I thought long and hard on if I wanted to continue with my devious plan. I mean the babies were part of me too. My phone started to vibrate, and I checked the caller id. It was Cherie's house phone. I answered it and it was my oldest son on the phone wondering why I wasn't at the shop when he arrived for our weekly outing. My head started to pound. I knew in that instance the babies that Geneva was carrying had to die.

"I love you son and don't worry daddy will be home to see you before the week is out. Alright soldier?"

"Yes daddy."

"Take care of your mommy and your brother and sisters. You the man while I'm gone. Got it?" I asked sternly.

"Yes, daddy, I a big boy and I got it."

"That's enough O.J. let daddy get back to his family."

"You are my family," I screamed hoping that my wife Cherie would hear me.

"Hang it up now," she said then all I heard was silence. I grabbed Geneva's plate and carried it into the living room and shook her.

"Damn, what's wrong?" she asked groggily.

"Nothing, your food's ready."

"I'm so tired I'll eat it later."

"Nope, eat it now while it's hot," I commanded.

I watched her pick at her food and made sure she ate it all by spoon feeding her the mashed potatoes.

Those babies are toast and I'm going back home to Cherie and my kids come hell or high water.

"I don't feel so good," she murmured. "What did you put in my food? I feel horrible."

"That feeling comes along with being pregnant."

"How do you know that?"

"Cherie would be as sick as a dog sometimes during her pregnancies."

"Cherie, Cherie, Cherie, I'm tired of hearing about the bitch."

"Well stop asking me questions then I won't have to respond. You know my world revolves around her and my family."

"Ugggh, I'm really feeling sick now," she said then commenced to vomiting. I looked at her secretly happy. She tried to get up and run to the bathroom but didn't make it in time. She threw up right outside of the door.

"God why do I feel so bad? Please don't let anything happen to my babies," she said as she felt a stream of water flow out of her. "Oh Lord, why me? Why me? These babies are not going to be able to survive."

"If they don't survive then they weren't meant to live," I said cutting off her last words.

She looked at me and I felt the daggers coming from her eyes. "What did you put in my food?"

"Nothing baby. The food just isn't agreeing with you plus judging by the blood and water flow down your leg, you're miscarrying."

"Oh no," she screamed and dropped to the floor crying. I secretly smiled inwardly; happy with my work.

"Come on, let me clean you up so I can call the ambulance," I said and rushed to her side to clean her up. I ran the bath water and told her to sit in the tub. I went back to grab her plate and threw the rest of her food out. I didn't want to leave any incriminating evidence.

"Hurry up. What's taking you so long?" she hollered.

"I'm coming damn," I answered. "Calm the fuck down before you put the babies in even more distress," I continued as if I cared. When I didn't get a response I went into the bathroom and seen her nodding off.

"Good," I mumbled under my breath. Her eyes popped open and she said, "Thank goodness you are here with me. Did you call the ambulance, what did they say, are they on their way?"

"No, I'm calling them now." She rolled her eyes and sucked her teeth. I decided to take my sweet time until she started yelling in angst and pain. I thought to myself, "Maybe I over did it with the pills. I don't want to kill her only the babies. Damn I hope this bitch don't die, but she has a history of pill popping so maybe the trail wouldn't lead back to me. At least I hope not. I was becoming a bit nervous and had to regroup. Geneva started to nod off again and I stood stuck in place watching her going through the motions. I thought about leaving her in the tub and just hauling ass to my mother's house so that I had a working alibi. After a few more minutes of watching her dose off I made the decision to call the ambulance.

"911 what's your emergency?""Yes, my girlfriend is nodding off. I believe she snorted some pills."

"Okay sir, did you say your girlfriend?"

"Yes."

"How old is she and what pills did she take?"

"She's 35 years old and I don't know the name of the pills she took. She usually pops Percocet and Xans."

"So your girlfriend has a history of snorting pills you say?"

"Yes, she has a history of abusing prescription drugs."

"Are there any other health ailments sir? Is she awake or coherent?"

"No, she's not fully awake. She keeps dozing off."

"Okay, let me get emergency medical techs on the line."

After a brief pause all I heard was, "Yes, I have a caller on the line who states his girlfriend keeps dozing off. He believes she has overdosed on some pills."

"I'm here, can you give me your exact location."

"Sure it's 2527 Bainbridge avenue apartment 2c."

"What are your cross streets?"

"I'm unsure."

"Ugggh, Omar, Omar, help me," came Geneva's weak cry for help.

"Hush, I'm on the phone with 911 now."

"Good, are they coming?""Yes," I said snidely rolling my eyes. The fuck she thought was going on….an audition?"

"Good, my whole-body aches and I'm so cold."

"She's probably about to go into shock," I thought to myself.

"Sir are you still there?"

"Yes."

"Sit them upright in front of a window where they can get some fresh air and if her condition changes in anyway, call us back for further instruction. EMTs' are on their way, so please lock up any animals that might perceive to be a threat and make sure your lights are on and the door is open to allow them entry. Do you understand my directives?"

"Yes. Yes, I do," I replied, and the call was disconnected.

I rushed back into the bathroom and helped Geneva out the tub. I patted her dry with a big fluffy red towel then proceeded to dress her. I propped her up on a chair in front of the window and made sure the front door was open. About ten minutes later the ambulance came and they assessed the situation. They placed her on a gurney and wheeled her to the back of the truck. I stood off in the distance.

"Sir are you coming?" an emt asked me. "If so, we need to get a move on it."

"No, no I'm not," I answered. I turned and went back in the house and closed the door. I peeked out the blinds and seen one EMT scratching his head and the other one trying to goad him into forgetting about me and do his job. It was a full five minutes before they pulled off. I looked around the house and realized what a mess it was I cleaned it with bleach and ammonia from top to bottom. I changed her sheets and threw them and her clothes in the washing machine. I laid down on the futon and drifted off into a disturbed peace.

"Why me? Why our babies? Omar, why did you do this to me?" Geneva said to me in my dreams.

"I didn't do anything to you Geneva. Stop lying and always trying to play the victim," I spat in her face. "And to take it one step further if you wouldn't have opened up your mouth to my wife about your kids then none of this would have happened. You opened the door with your big mouth now you suffer the consequences."

"So now it's not OUR kids anymore, but just MY kids? Boy you really know how to make a person feel special." "Fuck that. Feeling special comes with its prices and you my dear are paying full price. Now I'm going home to my WIFE and my KIDS. You take care," with that said I left her standing there feeling stupid. I truly didn't care. I awoke out of my dream to find I was still in Geneva's house. I checked my cell phone and the time read 12:19a.m. I scrolled through my contacts and called Cherie.

"Baby don't hang up just listen," I begged.

"You have three minutes."

"I don't love her like I love you and the children. I just want to come home to you and my babies. I promise I won't do this again. I don't like when you're hurting."

"Yes you do like it. If you didn't you wouldn't keep doing the same things over, over, and over again. Now would you."

"Baby look Geneva is in the hospital. I believe she is losing the babies. There's nothing left here for you to worry about. You are my wife and the only woman to have my children. I promise. Please just let me come back home. What do you say baby?" "I say your three minutes are over good-bye Omar," she said and hung up the phone. I called her back numerous times and she wouldn't answer my call. I put the phone down and felt the tears start to fall. After five minutes of me crying my phone started to vibrate. I didn't recognize the number but decided to answer the call anyway.

"Hello?" I answered hesitantly.

"They're gone," came Geneva's weak voice.

"Huh? Gone? Who and where have they gone?" I asked not fully believing her.

"The twins, they were still born."

"Oh okay, thank you for calling me."

"Thank you for calling? I just said your children were dead and that's all you have to say?"

"I never wanted those babies in the first place. Now that they are gone it is over between us. Don't expect me to be here when you are released," I said then hung up without waiting for a reply. "Fuck her and fuck her connect. I'll make one out in Philly," I thought to myself. I got up off the futon and looked around again and the house was spic and span. I got dressed and went searching her closet and dresser for items I once left here. When I was satisfied that I took all of my possessions I grabbed the keys to her minivan. "This bitch owes me this for telling my wife and causing me to be damn near destitute. I called my friend in Philly and asked if I could arrive a few days earlier. They said that would be fine, but before I headed out on the road I made a much-needed stop. This stop determined my next move I just hoped that all was forgiven.

CHAPTER 5

Three months later

Lord, I'm missing my husband. He's been gone for what seems like forever, but I can't forget the reason behind our separation. He was a dog and got that bitch Geneva pregnant. I can't believe I thought she was my friend. And although I know this may sound horrible, but I was happy as hell when he told me that she lost her twins. Sometimes I feel bad for being elated then other times part of me just doesn't give a fuck. There was an investigation as to if he gave her the pills that she overdosed on causing the twins to be stillborn but they couldn't prove it for sure. She had a history of popping pills before she even started to mess with my husband. She was even arrested for offering to give a blow job to an undercover cop in exchange for some pills and that was probably the only thing that saved him from being charged with their deaths. She called and harassed me for a while. Telling me things like Omar still calls her and says how much he loved her. And as always, I acted as if I didn't care. Truth is I do care. Omar has been a major part of my life for years and to have him suddenly not around was somewhat of a culture shock. Then I realized I had to love myself more than I loved anyone else or no one would love me the way I needed to be loved. I hope that makes sense. Even if it doesn't, the thought of loving myself more made me stand firm during the storm and my babies; my poor babies. The way their father was running around fucking like a dog in heat he could bring any type of venereal disease to me and shorten my life. What type of life would they have If both parents were to die from AIDS or Syphilis or some mess? As a result and every time I thought about it my resolve was strengthened.

While Omar has been away, I've invested my time in the children. I promised myself and them that I would make up for their father's absence. We did everything from store runs, to visiting amusement parks, museums and having picnics on Far Rockaway and Orchard beaches. We went to arcade rooms, played bowling, I even took them to a pool hall, during the day of course and we visited all types of movie theaters. There were days though when they wanted to know when their father was coming home. I would always lie and say soon. Truth is I don't know if and when Omar would be home. I was still debating on whether or not to tell him about the baby. I am due in three months, so I better hurry up and make a decision. I was only happy that the children didn't mention it to their father. I know there wouldn't be anything I could do to stop him from coming home should he find out and right now I'm still dealing with the negative feelings I have toward him about the Geneva incident. My mother says I need to get over it and move on. She also chastises me for not telling Omar about the new baby. All I can do is nod my head in agreement to her instructions. I mean I know I have to tell him. There's no way I can hide a whole baby from him forever, but for right now I have to try.

"Ma," Zera called out to me.

"What child?"

"The doorbell just rang."

"I didn't hear no door bell."

"Well it just rang. You want me to answer it?"

"Nah, I got it," I said and briskly walked out my bedroom and to the front door. I opened it without looking through the peep hole and by the time my eyes relayed to my brain what was happening, it was too late. All I saw was the flash from the gun's nozzle. I felt sharp pains all through my body knocking the wind out of me and I wound up falling on the floor.

Zera visibly shaken held her hands over her head and I saw another flash from the gun's nozzle then saw as she flew back from the impact of the bullet slamming into her little body. "Nooo," I screamed out and with all the strength I could muster I managed to kick our assailant. My foot connecting to their kneecaps dazed him for a second or two and I tried my best to kick them again. By this time Cameron started to scream at the top of his lungs and the assailant took one more look at me and Zera then fired three more bullets into my body and turned the gun toward Cameron. "No, he's just a baby," I shouted then immediately I blacked out after realizing there was more than one assailant. When I awoke I was in a hospital room and Omar was leaning over me crying.

"Zera and Cameron?" I managed to whisper causing Omar to go into hysterics.

"Nurse, nurse, she's awake. My wife is awake." A team of nurses and doctors flew into the room and started poking and prodding me to the point I had to ask them to stop.

"Hold on Mrs. Miller, let us do our job and make sure you are alright," a stern-faced nurse said to me.

"It's Roberson, not Miller."

"I'm sorry, but your husband said your name was Miller."

"That's my marriage name, but I filed for divorce about a week ago. I'd like to be referred to by my maiden name."

"You did what?" Omar said sounding hurt and shocked in the same breath.

"Yes, I filed for divorce."

"There's no way I'm allowing you to divorce me. Especially with the new baby and all."

"Baby," I said suddenly remembering I was expecting. My hands flew to my stomach area immediately. Something was wrong. "Where is the baby? Why don't I feel them moving or anything?"

"Well, we had to give you an emergency c-section, but we are optimistic that the baby, a girl by the way, is viable outside the womb, but we won't know for certain until all her test results are back from the lab. She's in NICU and if you behave and let us assess you properly I will personally wheel you down to the unit to see her."

"Would you?" I asked about to choke on the tears that were falling down my face. "Zera? Where is she? Did she survive? How about Cameron? They shot poor Cameron."

"Well, Cameron wasn't shot baby. He's a little shaken up and has been evaluated. He may need therapy, but he wasn't physically harmed. Zera was though," Omar informed me.

"Thank goodness the bullet must have missed him," I stated.

The doctor and Omar looked at each other as if stuck on stupid. "I'm going to ask one more time before I assume the worst. Where is my daughter Zera?"

"Sorry Mrs. Miller, I mean Roberson, Zera is in a medically induced coma. For now, all we can do is hope she responds to treatment."

That was all I needed to hear. I really couldn't hold back the water works. Tears flowed down my face while I could only wail out in agony. My mind flashed back to her being shot and falling backwards from the impact of the bullet once it hit her fragile petite body.

"Well please tell me that at least the perpetrators have been captured."

"At this time there aren't any witnesses baby," Omar said as he smoothed my kinky hair back in place.

"I can't believe this. Who could possibly hurt a five-year-old child? I mean she isn't bigger than two twigs intwined together."

"I know baby, but the cops have assured me that they will do everything in their power to capture the assailant."

"You mean assailants as in plural. Meaning more than one.""Wait, there was more than one including the getaway driver? Do you recall knowing any of them?"

"If there weren't any witnesses then how you knew there was a getaway driver?"

"The neighbor's security camera caught some images."

"Oh okay, yes there were more than one shooter and the getaway driver. There was something feminine about the second shooter, but then it all happened so fast I didn't know what was truly happening. I mean as soon as I opened the door they opened fired. My goodness. I managed to kick one of them, but I was hurting so I don't think I made much of an effect on them."

"Well, the police better find out who they are before I do because so help me God, I'm going back to my old days."

Who would want to hurt us so badly?" I wailed.

"Calm down baby," Omar tried to coax me.

"Calm down? Calm down? My baby was shot, I was shot, and poor Cameron is traumatized after seeing me and Zera shot and all you can say is calm down? How pray tell do you suggest I do that?"

I was on the brink of hysterics. The machines and monitors I was hooked up to started to beep like crazy. The machine was reading my blood pressure being 200 over 196.

"You have to calm down now or I will be forced to sedate you," the doctor warned me, but I just couldn't comply. I was hurting. After a few seconds when he realized that I wasn't calming down he gave the nurses the go ahead to administer me a sedative. At this point I didn't care what they did to me. If Zera and the new baby's conditions don't change, and they aren't expected to live then my life is over.

Then it dawned on me. I haven't heard or seen my other children.

"Omar, where are the children?"

"No worries, they weren't harmed. Thankfully when the police arrived and checked the house they found them fast asleep in their rooms except for Cameron."

"Oh no, where's Cameron? What happened to him?"

"He was in the living room crying over you and Zera being hurt, but he's in relatively good health physically."

"Thank goodness. I would die if anything happened to them.""Upon checking him over they found out he has Sickle Cell Anemia."

"No, no, no, why is everything bad happening to this family?""Baby, I wish I had all the answers, but I don't. What we can do now is follow the regimen and advice given to us by the hospital officials."

"I can't deal right now. I need this family healthy and I need Zera to pull through her injuries."

"I know you do. We both do, but just take it easy. The doctor and her team have everything under control."

"Who have the children?"

"My mother has the children. They will be safe with her. The police have a unit sitting outside her house until we find out a motive for this heartless attack."

"Good," I said, and Omar bent down to hug me and whisper in my ear.

"No matter what I say or how you may feel, I want you to know that I love you wholeheartedly. You are my world and if anything were to happen to you or our children, I would surely die. Because of this, I'm hoping the police hurries up and catches your assailants before word of who it really was get back to me because I'm going to come out of retirement and fuck shit up the way I used to do."

"No Omar, you left the bad boy life alone so that we could own our own businesses and raise our children void of everything that certain life comes with. Listen to me, I don't need you doing anything stupid. Please I need you to be free and alive in the street and I must admit at some point, I want you to come back home, but the womanizing has to stop. This time I was shot, next time it might be AIDS. You have to think with the head on your shoulders and not the head between your legs. Do you know I'm not ugly? Do you know that with children and all men still try and talk and flirt with me? I turn them down Omar. I turn them down and you want to know why? Because I love you and only you. There can never be a man to take your place. Not in my home, heart, with my children or between my legs. Those places are reserved for you my love and I mean this…. I love you and I only wish you loved me back."

"I do love you. What type of non-sense are you talking about? I love you Cherene Roberson and I wish you would take my last name."

"Omar don't start. I just told you all that you mean to me and your only rebuttal is something as simple as your last name? Please don't antagonize me."

"I'm sorry Cherie. I'm so sorry any of this is happening. I love you baby girl. For life!"

"For life? Or For now?"

"Stop Cherie. Stop with all these stupid questions. I love you more than I have ever loved any girl before and I'm only sorry that it almost cost you your life for me to realize it. I promise things will be better. I promise you that our Zera will be good as new and I promise you to always be a man that you can respect. One that you know loves you. Do you hear me baby girl?"I looked at him deep and intensely. I wanted to curse his ass out. It took us having all these children, me and our first born being shot and an affair which resulted in two dead babies for him to realize he loved me?

"Negro please get the fuck out of my room. You said you love me more than any other girl you have dated? Well therein lies the problem. I am a woman; not a girl. You have treated our bond, our relationship and our marital ties as a high school fling and here I am wondering why you don't love me? I see now that you are incapable of loving me on the capacity that you need to. On the level that I need to be loved. You, Omar Miller, are incapable of loving me whole body and soul and there is the problem. Now please, I'm only going to ask you one more time before I scream for hospital security, please get the fuck out of my room and my life for good. You don't love anyone else but yourself because you are incapable of loving me wholeheartedly. You disgust me so much. So very much and should I say this again…. you disgust me. I wasted all these years with you to only be looked at as a *girl* you love. Just great. Do you even know what love is? What it takes to make love work? Or do you have some preconceived notion that since you don't want me to die because of your lies that it must mean that you love me."

"What? Why are you flipping like this? What did I do to you?" he asked in total bewilderment.

"We had to go through all of this for you to realize that you loved me? I mean why did you even marry me? Was it just for the sake of you saying that you were married?"

He said nothing in return.

"Just what I figured. Get out my room."

"Baby please think about what you are doing. Don't push me away."

"Too late. You pushed your own self away the moment you broke our vows."

"What's it going to take for you to love and trust me again?"

"Who knows if I'll ever love and trust you again. I'm scarred for life and I think that we both know it was your transgressions that led to me and Zera being shot. So please, do me a favor, just know that you don't have to go home, but you got to get the fuck out of here. And I suggest you do it before I call security." With that said, I felt a ton of bricks being lifted from my shoulders. I felt the world shift and it was as if the weight of the world were on them. I know that I love my husband but I'm not sure if he feels the same and I'll never know, but I doubt it. It was that doubt that let me know I'd never trust him again. Now I have to trust myself and help my heart get over him.

He kissed me at the crown of my head and said, "I can't make you any promises. My Zera, my first born, was brutally attacked. I can't understand this. How and why did this have to happen to us?"

As soon as those words left his mouth I knew the answer. Now call me crazy and I wonder why I didn't bring this up before, but it was obvious who attacked me and my children. "Geneva," I said causing my mouth to go completely dry and Omar's eyes to open widely.

"Nah, she wouldn't have the heart," he said doubtfully.

"Never underestimate a scorned woman. Not only that, she always calling me threatening me. Now maybe she didn't pull the trigger, but I can guarantee you that she was one of the assailants. I am positive about this. I believe she was one of our attackers. There was something feminine about one of them."

"How so?"

"Just the stride she took back toward the getaway car. The lack of aim and precision on the gun that was trained on Cameron. What dude not gonna shoot straight?"

"You'd be surprised, but like you said don't under estimate a woman scorned so I won't under estimate her. If so, and she had any part in your attack, she better go hide back in her native country of Grenada because if she stays in the states, I'm killing her ass," he said looking as if he meant every word he had just spoken.

"I think you should go now," I stated calmly with my voice even and low although I was seething inside. He allowed another woman to harm us. He didn't even have enough balls to keep his ho in check so how the fuck could I trust him to exact revenge now. I had a nagging suspicion that he might have had a hand in our attacks. Maybe he wanted me and my children out the way so that he could live in peace with Geneva. And although I didn't want to think this was possible I never thought he would have children outside of our marriage either. He has shown time and time again that he is not one who should be trusted.

"I don't want to go."

"I need you to go. I need time to heal. Not only physically but mentally. This is all just so much to bear.

"Baby. I…"

"Sorry Mr. Miller," the doctor said cutting him off. "Your wife needs her rest. Plus, I have heard her ask you to leave numerous times, so please leave willingly or I will call hospital police," the doctor said crossing her arms in front of her as she stood with a visible attitude on her face. All I could think of was where the fuck did she pop out from because I swear as I talked to Omar no one else was in the room. I made a mental note to watch what I say around the hospital staff. They are known snitchers especially the Becky's of the hospital. I remembered the last time one called on me and Omar because I let it be known that I ran out of depression medication. We were investigated for months until they finally closed the case. They saw that we always had food in the house, the children were in day care, they were up to date with all their shots and there weren't any unexplainable bruises on their little bodies.

Turning my attention back on the matter at hand I listened intently as Omar started to talk.

"No, need for all of that. I'm leaving. I need to get to my mother's house and check on the children anyway," Omar stated then looked at me and says, "No matter what you may say, do or not do, just know I love you and I'm going to do everything in my power to right all the wrongs I've done to you."

"You're a male whore and I can't keep going through this with you. I almost lost my life and you still take up for the bitch that did the shit or put the wheels in motion."

"We don't know if it was her and I don't want to purposely put anyone in jail but the actual shooters."

"G.E.T. O.U.T. and I am not going to say it again," I shouted clapping my hands for emphasis.

"Now Mr. Miller. Leave now or I will press the security button," the doctor stated firmly without a trace or hint of a smile on her face.

"Alright, alright, I'm going, but just know I'll be back bright and early in the morning to check on you. Love you Cherie and thank you for your patience doctor."

He turned on his heels and walked briskly to the door, he stopped, turned to look at me and shook his head. He then proceeded to leave after holding back the words he wanted to say. Part of me cared about what he had to say, and the other part just didn't give a fuck. I knew in my heart that it would take a long time for me to get over all the pain he caused me. Sometimes I wish I didn't care as much, but I did. As this realization came to light in my mind, the tears flowed freely from my eyes.

"I'll leave you alone, so you can take a few minutes to compose yourself Ms. Roberson, but press the call button if you need anything. Anything at all," the doctor stated.

"Can you take me to see my Zera?"

"I'm not sure if I can, but I will try to do my best to have an orderly take you to her."

"Thank you doctor. That's all I ask."

With that said she nodded her head then left out of my hospital room. I continued to cry silently knowing that things in my household, with my family, will never be the same again.

CHAPTER 6

OMAR MILLER

After being put out of Cherie's hospital room I sat in the hospital's parking lot in my new 2017 Corolla. I lit up a cigarillo and commenced to taking deep puffs. I felt like the weight of the world on my shoulders was easing up. However, I was far from stupid and nowhere near naïve, so I know that not a damn thing changed about the position that I was in. I wanted to go see my baby girl Zera, but I just couldn't bring myself to looking at her again. I know that may be fucked up, but I know I'm the blame one way or another for her being in the predicament that she was in. Whether it was Geneva trying to get payback for the twins death or someone from my past when I lived a hustler's life. I did murk a few guys unbeknownst to Cherie. She knew I was a bad boy and but not how bad I was. I figured that what she didn't know would keep her and the children safe, but I guess I was wrong. Even though I have been out of that life for five years and counting it could still be a person's disgruntled loved one, but I was careful when laying niggas down. I never did dirt with anyone and any problem I had I handled it solo. And most importantly, I never, never, never, left any witnesses. So hell yea, some women and some teens were crucified. Due to these actions, I can't believe that it might be my past life coming back to haunt me. Looking into Zera's hazel eyes when she was born helped me decide to stay in school and stop all illegal activities, but you know the streets. No one is totally absolved for past sins and sometimes retribution is a must. I just hoped that my little girl's fighting spirit kicks in and she heals properly from her wounds. The doctor explained to me that a bullet just missed her heart and another one just missed her spine. I was so relieved because it seems as if God has bigger plans for her. "Doctor is she able to walk and talk?" I asked.

"I believe so, but I don't want to give you an official prognosis until she awakes from the coma and I'm able to fully assess her speech and motor skills," was her response.

Then my mind flashed unto parts of the conversation I had with Cherie. They kept playing and playing through my mind. Especially the part where Cherie stated that Geneva keeps threatening her. Could she have been the one that arranged the hit on my family or was it Simpson? Simpson was my plug for the illegal pills I was hustling in bulk on the side. I fucked up a package and he told me that it would be my ass. We got into a fist fight and he got the best of me, so I pulled out the strap and fired four shots. One hit him and the other hit his son. He pulled through, but his son is in a vegetative state. I know what he said but Simpson isn't a known bad boy, so I don't think he has the heart to retaliate. I mean I heard stories of how soft he was starting from when he was a young teen. Someone slapped his sister and he didn't even retaliate. Then his father exchanged words with a young man and told Simpson to fight him, but Simpson was afraid and asked his father not to allow the fight to happen. His father was so distraught he took off his belt and whooped Simpson in front of the passersby but when it comes down to the money and his own seed even the softest man might become hard. Upon further reflection, I decided to call Cream. She was a bad bitch who was Simpson's mistress. Well, at least one of the chicks he had on the side. She flirted with me every now and then and when alone she would purposely rub up against me, but I was trying to be a good man and win back my wife's favor after the first time she caught me screwing around. If anyone knew what Simpson was up to, it would be Cream. I might have to go after her under the illusion that I want to be with her. See I needed an inside connect and she would be the perfect person because of her affiliation to Simpson. I picked up my phone and scrolled the contacts. When I found the number I was looking for I pressed send and waited for the person to answer.

"Hello?" Cream said seductively.

"It's me Omar," I responded.

"Yes, I know who you are, but am unsure of the purpose behind your call."

"I need to know if possible can you meet me in New York City?"

"New York City? For what?" she asked in bewilderment.

"I think that what I have to talk to you about would be beneficial to the both of us. Yet it can't be discussed over the phone."

"Ah well, let me check my calendar and see if it's possible, but I'm not making any promises."

"Just do what you can, that's all that I ask."

"May I ask a bit of the details?""Details? I just said it can't be discussed over the phone," I reiterated in total amazement that she would still push the issue of me talking about the details over the phone. "Yes, I understand, but why do you want me to travel out of my way to meet you in New York City when you can meet me right here in Philly."

"What I have to talk to you about is top notch secret and I'm sure while you are here no one would be able to give the word back to Simpson that I was with you?""Ahh, I see. I'm supposed to keep this on the hush from Simpson?"

"Yes."

"Why?"

"Again, I can't really talk on this phone seeing as it's not a secured line."

"Say no more. I will be able to meet you in a week's time at the Econo Lodge in Co-Op City."

"Damn, you know New York City like that?""I know a lot of things that you would be surprised I know."

"Alright, alright. See you in a week's time and Cream?""Yes?"

"Don't stand me up. This is important. It's a matter of life and death."

"Don't worry. You have my word. I'll call you when I touch into town."

"Thank you."

"Don't thank me as yet. You never know if I have the solution to your problems."

"Oh, I believe you do."

We made a bit more random talk flirting back and forth with each other. By the time we hung up I almost forgot that I called her for the inside track as to if it was Simpson or not who put the hit out on my family. I couldn't tell from this particular phone call, but once I meet with Cream face to face I'm sure I will have the much-needed answers to my problems. I just prayed that God kept me sane until I could meet up with Cream. My baby girl deserved justice and I was going to be the one to give it to her; one way or another. Please believe me.

CHAPTER 7

I was in deep turmoil. One minute I'm filled with life in my belly then the next that life is gone. The doctor found massive amounts of Xanax, Percocet's and other highly addictive pain killers in my blood test such as Naproxen. They said it was a miracle that I was alive. While I didn't want to think the man I loved and who I was pregnant from would purposely try to kill me and our babies, I had no other choice but to believe it. Although a few of the details were foggy, I do remember asking for some pills to pop and he specifically told me no. So if I never willingly ingested the narcotics then I must have been fed them when he cooked for me and for that he had to pay; one way or another. So yes, I set up the hit on this nigga's beloved family, but who would have thought that Cherie and her pea of a child would be as tough as they are and somehow survive the murder attempt on their lives? Surely, I didn't think it was possible.

I also chided myself in missing the shot of Cameron. I mean he was right there in my line of fire, but for some reason my aim was off. I chalk it up to the little boy having angels surrounding and protecting him, but I really tried with everything in me to shoot that little booger snatcher. It was to no avail. Now I have Omar calling me all crazy asking me what I'm doing and if I went out of the house lately. He must think that I am stupid and that I would willingly tell on myself. Trust me I am not that stupid. I am very smart, or the police would have been put on to my scent already and charged me with attempted murder and that would be four counts because Cherie's bastard ass was pregnant and even that little crumb snatcher survived the attack. Yet my babies didn't. I'm hurt beyond repair and only the blood of their father and his other family will give me a peace of mind. I have to regroup and try this assassination shit again, but they have police units patrolling and sitting out front of Omar's mother's house, Cherie's parents house and Cherie and Omar's house as if they were presidential family and candidates. Now Omar has hardly been seen around the city, so I doubt that if we try this a second time that we would catch him. I am waiting for his anger to subside some and then I plan to get up close and personal to him. If need be I plan to shoot him myself in the midst of making love but in order to make love I need for my body to heal as well. Besides my immediate plans to quench my revenge for his blood. I have some real long, hard thinking to do because I have to decide if I am going to add police officers to my body count. These police officers are the ones that guard Omar and his mother's homes. I mean if we kill the officers then our plan has to be air tight. I am not going to face any outrageous charges that killing an officer would bring to us. We have to play this smart. It seems as if the police rotate circling Cherie's block every five through ten minutes and they sit permanently there from 11 pm through the morning until 6 am. If we are to retaliate again then it would be best to do so around those times to eliminate the possibility of eye witnesses. Then there are also the officers body cameras and dashboard cams. We can always come up from behind them and shoot them, but I'm thinking that some sort of scrambler could be used to mess with the dash and body cams. Maybe we can catch a cop coming from a rest room break and instruct him to turn off his body cam.

All of my ideas play out nicely in my head and I'm sure that some if not all of them could work if executed properly. However, I can't get my brother Fox to agree with me on this matter. He says it's stupid to do so and that our best bet is to catch Omar slipping by himself as he has been known to do when he rides around the city solo. Although he made a few valid points I am adamant that I want Omar dead along with the rest of his family. That is something Fox is not willing to take another chance on and feels we should just kill the man responsible for killing my babies. I informed Fox it was smart to do so. When he asked my reasoning I said because although they have cops guarding the place they don't really expect lightning to strike in the same place twice. After some prodding my brother told me that I might be onto something, but that if we play our hand right we can catch Cherie and the family when no cops were around. He said he bets that the cops will only be guarding the place for about two more weeks until they feel it's safe and that we won't be coming back around. I had to agree with his logic, but then I told him, "If in two weeks' time the cops are still guarding that nigga's house and his family I'm going there at 2 am, bodying the cops and everything in the house that's breathing."

"Damn sis. What really has this nigga done to you?""He killed my babies."

"There is no conclusive proof that he did."

"Oh so you don't believe me either?"

"Not that I don't totally believe you. There's just no concrete proof for me to fucking believe you," he said showing his frustrations."Well fuck you then. I got this. I don't need your help."

"Sure you do."

"How do you figure?"

"Because your ass can't shoot for shit," he said then fell out laughing."I can so shoot."

"No you can't. Guns make you nervous."

"No they don't."

"Yes they do."

"How do you figure?"

"I saw your hands shaking when you had a clear and concise shot. You just couldn't seal the deal and your temperament that night shows you shouldn't have no parts of any mass shooting."

"But it's not like your bullets did their job."

"My bullets hit though. I don't shoot to miss. Not like you do at least.""What's your problem?"

"I don't have a problem. Do you?""Yes, I have a problem. No one died."

"Honestly this whole shit is whack to me, but you're my baby sis and when you hurt I hurt. Now I tried to do this hit your way. I brought the beef to their motherfucking door and aired shit out. You said you wanted the nigga to feel pain. He's feeling it. Now I know dude from back in the day. He may have went to college and own a business or two, but trust don't sleep on him. The cops are just a front, but I bet he has something big up his sleeve and I feel sorry for who ever he unleashes on. Now I say before it reaches that point you listen to me, another real street nigga and let me air Omar out before he airs us out. You'll thank me in the long run."

"No, I want him to suffer and I need for it to be one of his children or his beloved wife.""Ahh, I see what this shit is."

"You do?"

"Yes. It has nothing to do with the dead babies."

"It has everything to do with MY DEAD BABIES," I yelled. "Don't you see Fox? Don't you see they were murdered? And then he rushes to his wife's side and not mine when I'm hurting," I said now screaming in hysterics.

"Like I said, I see what this is."

"What is this then? What is it? It is about my dead babies and you can't tell me shit otherwise."

"You all in your feelings because he chose another bitch over you. Now you might say it's about them dead babies and I admit a nigga was wrong to kill his own seeds, but it's really about the wife having his favor over you. You can't take it and now you are unraveling. May I be honest with you sis?""Sure, you've been this honest for so long."

"I say give it up. Give up this pipe dream of killing his family and having the nigga all to yourself. Chalk the babies up to the game and find someone to move on in life with. You are far from ugly, plus you are intelligent. You should find another man in no time. See the way I see things is he already showed you he could care less about having a future with you. I mean come on you keep saying he killed the babies. He could have killed you too and moved on with his life without anyone being none the wiser. He doesn't love you and I'm sorry to tell it to you plain and simple like that, but he doesn't. I'm a man and I know that no one or nothing and no one could make me kill my babies and if they did then the person who was carrying those babies was a mutt to me. And I mean that as honest and plain as I could so that you could understand. Give it up sis. He's just not in love with you and that's the God's honest Truth."

"Gee thanks."

"Don't 'gee thanks' me. Move on and show me that you are recouping and above all know that I love you and I only want the best for you so I'm not going to lie to you. Call me whenever you need me but give up this pipe dream of murking O's family. So far, we seem to have gotten away with the first attempt because it was unexpected. Next time, we may not get caught but something worse can happen."

"Something worse than getting caught? My babies were murdered. I'll do whatever it is to bring them justice. And while it may not be YOUR definition of justice, it is something more powerful."

"More powerful than justice?" my confused brother said.

"Yes, you should know this."

"I don't have time for the guessing game. I know one thing You may not get away with a second attempt, but you might be the next to leave this world instead. I'm trying to stop that from happening. Let's give this up while the going is good. For both our sakes," he said somewhat scaring me.

Tears flowed down my face like a river raging when a dam broke. I knew what my crazy ass brother was saying was gospel, but I wasn't ready to admit that thought out loud. And my brother was crazy. Hence the nickname Fox. It came from the saying, 'Crazy like a Fox.' But he wasn't living up to the saying. However, in my heart I knew that if something was too far-fetched for Fox to attempt then the end goal had to be unattainable but I'm not willing to throw in the towel as of yet. I wanted him to go with the flow and tell me he would help me murder Omar's family and anyone who stood in our way even if it were the police, but he just wasn't giving that to me. Now I know that my brother is wild and crazy as they come, but if even he were giving Omar his due respect then I know that Omar is not someone I truly wanted to fuck over, but I can't just let my two dead babies go out like that. I had to get Omar back for the degradation and pain he caused me and next time I won't mess up.

"Excuse me a minute sis," Fox said as he checked his vibrating phone. "Yea, hello?" he said and listened intently while I could hear a girl's voice screeching through his ear piece.

"What the hell is that all about?" I asked curiously.

"Hush," he said to me then turned his attention back to the phone. "No, not you. I'm with my sister Geneva. Now as you were saying."

I tried to listen as best as I could as he tried to soothe the apparently crying female. "I'll try my best to get to the bottom of this matter. Don't worry. His death will not be in vain."

"Now what?" I mouthed to him and he held his finger over his mouth in another attempt to shush me.

As soon as he hung up the phone call I was all in his ear. "Who was that and who died? I asked in one breath.

"You not going to believe this, but Justin was just killed."

"Justin, the driver?"

"Yes, Justin the driver and his wife is in hysterics. She said that the last lick he was in on was with us and if we know anything about who might have wanted him dead? She also wanted to know could this be retaliation for the last lick we did?"

"How would Omar find out so fast who the players in the failed assassination was? And who he have that would be willing to kill Justin?"

"You still don't get everything I've been saying to you have you sis? I know you had some learning problems growing up, but I always thought you were street smart. Not only that, but I have been telling you for the past hour and a half why you should give up your plans to try and murk O's family again but you still not grasping the severity of the situation. Now for the last time please think with your head on your shoulders and not the heart beating in your chest."

"I'm listening to you, but I can't understand what about Omar have people shook."

"Damn Gee, you don't get it. Let me put it to you like this. If you continue to go after Omar's family I will not help you at all. You are completely on your own. You get your own people to help you because me and my crew is out of this. We have children and wives to live for. Now I'm sorry your children are dead, but I no longer want a part in your bullshit."

"Damn! Bullshit? Is that they way you see the life of your niece and nephew?"

"They weren't even born alive. They didn't feel any pain. You didn't even get a chance to know them, hold them, feed them, have a birthday party for them. They were fetuses; not babies. Now give it up. This revenge stream you are on will not work. Not against someone of Omar's caliber. I love you. You're my sister but I have children to live and provide for. I wish you the best and I will check on you in a few days to see if you have calmed down. If not Gee, you are entirely on your own and I mean this," Fox said getting up from my butter colored leather sofa. He finished drinking the last of his beer and set the can back down on the coaster on the coffee table, kissed me in the top of my head then headed toward the front door to make his exit. "Come lock up this door and get some rest because you look like shit."

"Gee, thank you Fox."

And that was the last time I looked at my brother with any ounce of respect.

CHAPTER 8

OMAR MILLER

Cherie may have thought I was taking this lightly. She may have even thought I was being naïve or taking up for Geneva. Truth of the matter is I'm not. Besides my meeting with Cream I have my feelers to the ground and the streets are talking. They gave up Justin as having a part of the attack of my innocent baby girl Zera. Well sort of, they said he has been acting funny lately and as if he came into a bit of money when just a few days ago he was picking up half smoked cigarette clips from the ground and begging people for dollars on the train. He now had a new hoopty, similar to the one seen outside of Cherie's house the day of the attack. That was all I needed to hear. Although I couldn't help but to wonder where Geneva got the money to pay him. Then I remembered she had told me she had a nice little savings from the allowances that I used to give her. Plus she did sell her cherry red 2015 fully equipped Lexus truck. I thought she had put everything back into the new mini-van that she bought to knock around in since she was pregnant with the twins, but she didn't. The blue book value on the van was way less than her Buick. So it seemed she has some money lying around. I guess she used that to pay him.

It was easy to get to Justin. He was a creature of habit, so I waited for Justin in front of Smiley's bodega. I watched his mannerisms as he realized it was me in front of the store. "Need a dollar? "I asked him being funny.

"Nah, I'm good. I got it."

"Since when?" I asked prying.

"Look man I said I'm good," he stated trying to avoid looking in my eyes. Right then I knew this grimy, greasy nigga had a hand in hurting my family. So I went in for the kill to obtain the knowledge that I already knew.

"Did you hear what happened with my family?" I asked paying close attention to him. His eyes started to jump, and he started to stutter.

"Nah…nah…nah…I ain't hear nothing."

"Word? Because that's all the streets keep whispering about. I mean everywhere I go people are telling me they are sorry for what happened to my baby girl. They even say that your car you driving there was seen outside my house. So tell me. What happened to my family?" "Aye man, I don't know nothing about nothing and I don't know why people trying to trip me up in that bullshit."

"Bullshit? Are you sure this is the way you want to play things?"

"Again, I don't know anything."

"Okay. You take care," I said and callously tossed the cigarette I was smoking. I went to my car then drove down the block slowly. I watched him watch me drive away. I pulled into the twenty-four-hour parking lot and positioned myself to follow him after he drove past.

It took about three minutes for him to speed past me. I thought to myself he must be the easiest mark I've had in a while. He took me back to my murderous days. People knew once I approached them their imminent demise was on the way. After following him for about fifteen minutes he pulled into a driveway. I pulled right up blocking him. I rolled down my passenger car window and our eyes locked. He was able to mouth, "Oh shit," then his dome split and brain matter popped back onto his paved driveway. "Bulls eye," I yelled then pulled away. I drove for about an hour upstate to a chop shop I deal with. I pulled the Chevy Camaro in and drove a Mercedes truck out. It felt good having access back to my money. Although Cherie didn't give me full access back I did have use of the bank account to run errands for her and I have been taking care of the babies while her, the new baby and Zera, who was now fully awake from her coma, healed from their wounds. My only dilemma was how and when to get at Geneva. I wanted her to suffer nice and slow. I know I was a motherfucker when I made her lose the twins, but my thing is take that shit out on me not my family, but she didn't. Now I must make her pay and she will do so with every bit of her being. I was going to make her the last one to die but next on my hit list was Fox. The streets say he was the first and main shooter and for that he was going to pay with his life, but before that happened I had my meeting with Cream. Although I know that Simpson didn't have anything to do with the assault on my family I wanted to meet with her. I know that I shouldn't be thinking about another mistress but there was something about her that was just so sexy it was drawing me to her. I was a bunch of raw nerves and I needed some sexual healing to calm me down. Even if Cherie wanted to fuck around she couldn't, and I figured a little taste of Cream wouldn't hurt. I wasn't going to trust her fully like I did Geneva only to be played with. I was going to get the skins then scram. Sex once or twice with no strings attached while Cherie was healing. Call me a dog but I just had to have some of Cream. She was the thing that my dreams are made of and I wanted to taste her.

CHAPTER 9

"Crazy like a fox," came Roberta's sleek voice from behind the door as she looked through the peephole before opening it up.

"Yes, that's me baby."

"Had a rough day?" she asked seductively.

"No rougher than usual. Why?"

"I heard what happened to Justin. Should I be worried?" my wife asked me.

"Listen, I got tripped up in some bullshit, but I think we cool."

"Well Cynthia is about losing her mind and I'd hate to be in her position. So we should just prepare for to head down south for a while."

"I can't leave. I have a few more things lined up."

"This better not have anything to do with your sister."

"Nah, we cool on that. She knows where I stand."

"Where do you stand Fox? I don't want to lose you."

"I stand with you baby. Let me just pull a few loose strings and tie them neatly then we'll go away for a while. How about Aruba? This time of year it's beautiful and we can take a siesta."

"Baby, you know I love Aruba. Let's go tonight."

"We can't just pick up and leave like that. The children, school and we don't need CPS knocking back on our door."

"We don't need the likes of Omar knocking on it either."

"Omar may be a lot of things but don't forget that my name garner just as much respect in these streets as his does. Now we'll leave in two weeks once I tie up a few loose ends and don't question me again."

"Whatever you say Fox," she said getting up and throwing a wet paper towel at me that she used to dry off the table she was cleaning with Windex and water. Stopping short, she turns and stares me deep in the eyes, "I don't want to lose you. I can't say this enough. You are not only my husband and father of my children, you are my best friend. You are the man who raised me once my parents were killed. You filled their shoes and those were mighty big shoes to fill. You took me from foster care and loved on me. You put me in this house and made it my castle. You treat me like a Queen and you have me on this pedestal and I don't want to come down and that's exactly what will happen if you run behind your sister and this vendetta she has for Omar."

"What do you know about my sister?" I questioned stupidly.

"The streets talk and although you are my world my sister is in that world and she tells me things."

"Oh really?" I said scrambling for something more tangible to say.

"Yes, really and I know that if you keep running behind your sister because of some dead babies you will end up dead and I don't know how or if me and your babies can make it without you."

"Just one more loose end baby. That's all; that's it," I said acknowledging not only to my wife but myself that I was going to try one more assassination attempt on Omar and his family in two weeks when the cops will more than likely end their guarding of him.

"One more loose end? Are you serious? Are you fucking serious? Tying up one more loose end can not only get you killed but get us killed as well. Don't you get it baby? This is bigger than you. He is bigger than you. He's Omar baby and you don't just shoot those he love and think he will let you live. Hell, you don't say 'boo' to those he loves and live. It's not as simple as you are trying to make it out to be."

"I love you baby and I'm sorry you don't have faith in me like you used to. But you have my word that if I can't successfully end this nigga's life in two weeks then I'm out the game."

"I knew it. I knew you were going to go after him."

"Well you said yourself that you don't just shoot those he loves and expect to live. I mean he already killed Justin so it's just a matter of time before he tries to kill me or even you and the kids and I can't have that. So I have to do this nigga in or we'll never be safe; not even in Aruba," I said halfway admitting defeat.

 I picked up the phone and called Geneva.

"What?""Two weeks; we get in, hit the nigga then get out and I don't want to hear no more about it. Understand me?"

"Yes, bro; loud and clear."

"Good. Now I'm spending time with my family. Why don't you go out with aunty Rayah or something? Do some girly shit and try to take your mind off them babies. I love you and don't say that your bro never comes through in the clutch."

"I won't, and I love you too."

"Peace," I said hanging up before she got the chance to answer. I might regret my decision, but I knew as well as my lady knows that a nigga like Omar is on a vendetta and if I don't get to him before he gets to me then I'm as good as toast. We touched his family; his pride and joy and for that he has to make us pay. He already killed one of us and there were only two of us left to get; me and Geneva. This was no longer about those two dead babies but more so about my black ass; my fine ass but black never the less and I didn't want to die another statistic of black on black crime.

"Nigga got to go and that's that," I said hyping myself up and reaching to light another cigarette. I watched Roberta's sexy ass walk past me and I decided I wanted to frolic a little. "Bring that ass here baby. I need some loving."

"And I'm going to give it to you," she said and pranced her voluptuous ass back in the living room. She straddled me and pushed me back on the fluffy sofa cushions. She stuck her tongue deep in my throat and proceeded to kiss me with as much fervor as she could muster. I kissed her back and unsnapped her bra releasing her perky, brown titties.

I grabbed one of her nipples with my mouth and gently suckled it while playing with the other one. She reached for my zipper and released my member from its bondage. She lifted her satin pink nightgown up and pulled her hot pink thong to the side. She sat on my dick and we grinded together in a smooth rhythmic motion until we both came and collapsed within each other. The sound of our two-year-old baby Thomasina broke us from our current position.

"That was good baby. Love you," I said to her.

"Love you back."

"Forever?"

"Forever Fox," and with that said she got up to tend to our children and I laid in the same spot we sexed, wet and all and fell into a deep troubled sleep. I dreamt Omar got the drop on me and was chasing me down a long corridor when out jumped Geneva and instead of busting a cap in his ass she shot me, and they walked away hand in hand like two love birds. I woke up dripping with sweat. I wiped my brow and whispered, "This bitch best ta not play me or else," and I left the rest of my thoughts at that.

CHAPTER 10

CHERENE 'CHERIE' ROBERSON

One Week Later

I wasn't at one hundred percent, but I had stayed the extent of what my health insurance was willing to pay out, so the doctor was releasing me to outpatient care. As for Zera and the new baby they would be in the hospital for a spell. Zera was healing but she was less than half-way healed, and the new baby was expected to live but hadn't reached a weight that the doctor's felt comfortable enough to release her into my care. They did say that even when she was released she would need home care assistance. I was hoping and praying that was approved by the health insurance as well.

As for Omar, he came and went every day. The more I told him to stay away the more he seemed to keep coming. I couldn't blame him though. For all intents and purposes we are his family and I had no conclusive proof that he planned to harm me along with Geneva. While I hoped not, I did financially cut his ass off and people do strange things for some change and yes that even means killing their loved ones.

"Peekaboo," came Cameron's little voice.

"Peekaboo baby come give mommy some hugs and kisses," I said scooping him up in my arms. I planted little wet kisses all over his face and upper body. He giggled and squealed in delight and I giggled too. We were enjoying our moment when my phone rang. I looked at the caller i.d. and realized it was Geneva's dirty ass. I sent her straight to voicemail and made a mental note to call the detective who spoke with her the last time and tell him that the harassing phone calls have started back up. In the meantime I was going to enjoy my children and every moment I could spend with them. They almost lost me and so I was going to make it my business to let them know how much I love and need them in my life and I wouldn't allow anyone else to come in between our moments. As soon as my phone stopped ringing for the fourteenth time the doorbell rang, stopping my heart.

"Ma, door," Cameron said equally disturbed.

"Hush. Cameron you stay here. Mommy will get the door." I went into the lock box that Omar gave me to hold a firearm. I nervously opened the lock and grabbed the shiny new pistol. I looked at Cameron once more and placed my finger up to my mouth in order to shush him and make him be quiet. "Stay here and stay put," I whispered to him. I edged out of my bedroom door and closed it behind me hearing Cameron immediately start to cry. I stopped midway and was torn on if I should go back and comfort him and let whoever was at the door stay on the other side or continue going so that I could see if we were in harm's way. My gut told me to keep going and before I could peek out the blind I heard Omar banging on the door, "It's me baby, don't be scared." I breathed a sigh of relief. I flung open the door and started to cry.

"What's wrong baby? What's wrong? Did somebody come back here?"

"I thought I was strong enough."

"Strong enough?" he asked me confused.

"I thought I was strong enough to stay in my house but even with armed police I am frightened. I can't stay here anymore Omar."

"And you don't have to. You can stay at my mother's house."

"No, I don't know if I can stay in the city. Take me with you to Philadelphia."

"When Zera and the new baby is released from the hospital we can leave but right now we need to stay as close to the hospital as possible. I know you're scared but I will stay here with you."

"You can----"

"Before you tell me what I can and can't do I will sleep on the sofa and I won't try and come in the bedroom at all. I promise. Let me make this right."

"Okay," I reluctantly gave in after a moment's hesitation. It will make me feel more safe to have Omar at home and I did have to stay close for the children's sake. I wouldn't be able to bear it if I had to live all the way in Philly and couldn't get back and forth to visit with them at any time I chose to.

"What are you thinking about?" Omar asked me interrupting my thoughts.

"That I would feel more safe with you in the home."

"Our home," he corrected me.

"I'm putting this home on the market. There's no way I'd feel safe here anymore and you have to work so you won't always be here to protect us. I can't live with this fear."

"Maaaaa," came Cameron's terrified voice and I jumped from Omar's embrace to go console him.

"I'm here baby; I'm here," I said rushing to pick him up. I smoothed his growing hair back from his face. "My baby needs a haircut!" I said thinking out loud.

"I'll cut it for you. Where are the clippers?" asked Omar.

"In the same place you always leave them."

"You want me to give him a baldie or line him up nicely."

"Line him up. Make him look extra sharp. He starts preschool tomorrow."

"Are you sure he should be away from us right now baby?"

"I want the children to have a sense of normalcy."

"Yea, but it isn't normal. He hasn't even attended a day yet. So he truly doesn't realize what he is missing."

"You're right and no, I don't want my baby to be away from me for a moment until our attackers are caught."

"Me either."

I moved in close and hugged him tight with all my might. He smelled so good but that was as far as I would allow myself to get close to him. He kissed me on top of my forehead and said, "Put Cameron to sleep and let me eat your pussy baby."

"No, how could you even fix your mouth to say such a thing."

"Because I miss you."

"I know but not now. Now is not the time. We are in this position because you couldn't keep your dick and head game at home. I refuse to fall victim to your sex again."

"It's nothing wrong with showing my woman I love her."

"That's the problem. You were showing your woman how much you love her when you had a whole wife at home," I said and mushed him in his face breaking our embrace.

"I'm going to make you love me again. Just watch!"

I can't front the thought of his head between my legs and his tongue on my pearl made me shiver with chills, but I refused to be stupid. I have been stupid for so long. It was time for me to smarten up and tighten up while I am at it and that means not sexing Omar simply because he asked for it. I had to be stronger than what I've been so that no one would ever think to attack my Homefront again and that's word to everything I love.

CHAPTER 11

OMAR MILLER

I was crushed Cream called me and said she couldn't give Stone the slip in order for her to get away and make a quick trip to New York City. I guess everything fell in line for a reason because when I showed up at the house Cherie was a bundle of nerves. I realized that my selfish desires needed to be placed on the back burner because the person who I loved more than most needed me most and when I heard poor Cameron crying my heart strings tugged something awful. Cherie was talking about him needing a haircut and I realized that my home life had to be put before some pussy. So that's what I did; cut Cameron's hair and rubbed Cherie's feet while she dozed off and took a well-deserved nap. She awoke a few hours later to put dinner on and we all sat at the large white marble dining room table like old times minus the noticeable absence of Zera who the mouth was usually most heard. Cherie teared up a bit and I kept on talking like I didn't notice anything was wrong. My main goal was to take Cherie's mind off our baby girl's absence but I'm not sure I succeeded but I tried my hardest.

"Baby this roast taste so good. Did you try something different?" I asked making small talk.

"Actually, it's your mother's recipe. I used gravy master instead of regular browned flour."

"Well, it tastes good. Not quite like my momma's but close."

"Of course. No one can throw down in the kitchen like your momma. I must admit I come close but not close enough."

"Ain't that the truth," I concurred and we both fell out laughing.

"What funny?" Cameron asked in his little baby voice.

"Nothing man," I said knowing he wouldn't quite understand. Cherie looked at me and we both shrugged our shoulders.

"You want more meat man?" Cherie asked Cameron.

"No, sleep."

"Tired? I'll put you in the bath and lay you down."

"Good," he said causing Cherie and I to laugh once again. Man I missed these times with my family. I thought about the dead babies briefly but decided not to chastise myself over them. They were in a better place. I wouldn't have been able to parent them the way I do my children I have with my wife and no one can fault me for not wanting to co-parent with the side chick. No one with good sense anyway.

"What are you so deep in thought about?" Cherie asked me breaking through my thoughts. "I'm sorry that I hurt you."

"Don't start," she huffed.

"But you asked."

"I know but I wouldn't have if I knew what you were really thinking about."

"At some point we need to discuss the pain I caused you."

"We have discussed it and it landed you living in another state."

"When the children are healthy enough to relocate we can all live out of state."

"So I can have some new hoes to contend with for your attention and time? No thank you."

"Why does everything have to be about hoes?" "Since you made it that way. Listen, I'm putting Cameron down for bed now. You know where the linen is. Make yourself comfortable and if I feel up to it I will come down and we can try speaking again but please no talks about you loving or hurting me. I can't bear those conversations. Okay?"

"Okay, baby. Love you."

"There you go," she chided me. "All I said was I love you."

"That hurts."

"How does me loving you hurt?"

"See this," she said removing her shirt strap so that I could see her wound that was covered in gauze. "This is how your love hurts me and will continue to hurt me as long as I am breathing."

"Goodnight Cameron," I said totally changing the subject and making a mental note to not tell my wife that I love her for fear of hurting her even more than I already have. The last thing I wanted to do was continually hurt her. So if I couldn't tell her that I loved her then so be it.

CHAPTER 12

OMAR MILLER

It has been two weeks since Cherie has been home from the hospital. The new baby was due home from the hospital any day. It was my hope that Zera would be strong enough to leave the hospital as well but that just isn't the case. If my calculations were correct and the way I know Fox like I think I know Fox then he should be planning to hit my house soon. Try as I might to get an exact routine down for him, so I could hit him first I just wasn't able to do so because Cherie was more dependent on me than I originally thought she would be. With the armed police guards here guarding us I didn't have too many qualms, but the police chief has given specific orders for all vehicles to return to active patrol. They feel that my family is out of the woods and no one would be stupid enough to try and attempt to murder them once again. I, being the street cat that I am, know better. As a result, I dipped into Cherie's bank account and withdrew sixty-five thousand dollars. I used that to pay a few street thugs to guard my house. I told them if Fox or anyone suspicious came to my front gate to lay their asses out and we'll sort out the detail later.

I was confident with the two dudes I put on my payroll. One was named Shiloh and the other Iggy. They were both wild and crazy cats who used to run with me and Fox back in the days. I knew I could trust them because them and Fox came to blows over some money and drugs. Fox shot up their new stash house and they haven't been able to exact any revenge on his ass yet. Seems he's been laying low. That's why I knew he had something planned for my ass. I know how he thinks. And these two cats I had on my team were chomping at the bits to do him in. It was only a matter of time. My hiring them gave them just the opportunity they needed plus they made thirty thousand dollars and new state of the art infra-red beams each to sit around and wait on his ass to act. It was a clear win/win situation for them.

Ring…ring…ring…ring….

"Hello," I said answering a call from a private phone call which I don't usually do but given the times I had no choice to be picky.

"You don't even call to see how I'm doing. The babies died, and your ass don't seem to care."

"How the fuck do I know they were even my babies. I mean if you sleep with one man knowing he had a wife at home who the hell else would you sleep with," I came at Geneva sideways.

"Are you sure you want to play with me like this O?" she queried.

"Do I sense a hint of a threat in your question?" "It ain't a threat but let's just say if I shoot this time I won't miss."

"You're going to regret you said those words. I'm going to make you suffer nice and slow. Trust me. I won't be gentle."

"Fuck you and your little family. It's nothing to get you touched," she said slurring her words. "I see you've been drinking so now you have some liquid courage. You won't have that for long. Soon as the liquor runs out so will the heart hiding in your mouth. Trust me."

"Trust me. Trust me. That's all you can ever say," she said trying to mock me. I heard all I needed to hear from her, so I hung up the phone. She called me numerous times leaving weird little threatening messages. I paid her no mind and went back to the task at hand…unloading these pills I was supposed to give to her connect to the Crypt Keepers. I charged them $550,000.00 as opposed to the $400,000.00 I was supposed to. Hell fuck it, I needed every dime I could get to replenish Cherie's bank account. Things have been tight since I had to hire a new staff member at the store. I was trying to do everything I could to make Cherie's life as comfortable as possible and I didn't want her to be having to worry about standing on her feet in the pharmacy all day. It felt good to be back at work in my own store and although Cherie removed my name from the ownership papers it's like I never left. I called my friend from Philadelphia and told him I'd return once things were situated with my family and given the situation of course he understood.

"Hey boss man," Shiloh said to me when I returned home from the pharmacy.

"Everything quiet?" I asked him.

"Nah we had a little activity."

"What kind?"

"A blue Le Sabre has been driving through the block. I would have thought nothing of it, but it circled through more than once."

"Okay, good looking. Here's the Popeyes dinner box you asked for. Why don't you eat, and I'll sit out here with you two guys while you grub."

"Sure thing. Say, how do you want us to handle the Le Sabre?"

"Did you get a good look at the driver?"

"No, not really."

"Well try that first and we'll take it from there."

"Sure thing," he said taking a bite out of his dinner. I watched as he and Iggy devoured their meals. I made a mental note to leave the shop during lunch hours and bring them heroes and chips during the day. To be on guard they need to be on point and not have to worry about rumbling stomachs.

"Why so quiet boss man?" Iggy asked me. "Honestly? I don't like feeling like a sitting goose, so we have to come up with a way to draw Fox from his hiding spot, so we can body his ass. My family shouldn't have to be used as bait."

"Good, I thought you'd never suggest it. We can----" Shiloh started.

"Oh shit, they busting at the house," Iggy interrupted.

Wasting no time I reached down to my ankle and pulled my baby glock out. Aiming with precision I hit the driver on the side of the head.

"Foxxxxxx," came Geneva's cry.

I reloaded and got out the car.

"Wait," came Shiloh's voice.

"Nah, fuck that," I said and trained my gun on Geneva.

"O no. Don't do it," came my wife's voice.

"Bitttchhhh!!!" Geneva screamed out.

"Get down Cherie," I called out and all I heard was gunfire as Cherie dropped to the floor.

"Nooo," I said as I turned my gun on Geneva her head busted open and blood and brain matter flew everywhere.

"Bullseye," Shiloh said then rushed to me and grabbed my gun. "Go in the house boss man. We'll take care of this mess.

I raced up my front steps and turned back to see Iggy pushing Fox's dead body over. I heard sirens in the distance as Iggy sped away with Geneva halfway hanging out the window. I prayed silently for all our sakes that Iggy was able to outdrive the cops that were fast approaching. "Omar," came Cherie's weak cry.

"My god baby are you hit? Where'd the bullet hit you?""I'm not hit; I dropped to the floor when you told me to get down," she said bewildered.

I let out a hearty laugh as the cops flew past the house with sirens blaring.

"Are they dead?""Who baby?""Don't fucking play with me. You know who," she said upset.

"Yes, honey I believe they are dead."

"Good, what happens now?""Now, Shiloh and Iggy take the bodies and car to be disposed of and we never speak of this incident again."

"Are we in the clear?"

"Yea, I'll round up the surveillance tapes from the neighbors, who by the grace of God are on vacation so they'll just think it was a robbery attempt on their house."

"How will you manage that?""The less you know the better."

"You're right."

"I know, and I love you baby girl."

"I love you too," she said throwing her arms around me which was a sudden change from the other times she told me not to tell her I love her. "I hope things go back to normal."

"They're dead now baby. Things will go back to normal," I said feeling my cell phone vibrate in my pocket. "Come on, let's get up off the floor and go check on the children."

"I'll go. You make sure the coast is clear."

"Okay baby," I said relieved that she was fine. I watched as she went to check on our children. I felt in my heart that with Geneva dead and gone things between me and my wife will heal. I swore to myself that I would put one hundred percent into my marriage then my phone vibrated again. It was a text message. *"Hey Omar, I finally gave Stone the slip. I can meet you tomorrow at ten p.m. just to make sure I'm not followed. Is that good for you?"*

"Damn," I said to myself. *"Maybe one more mistress won't hurt………………"*

THE END